For Sandro Botticelli who inspired the fairies. A.M.

The Midsummer Bride is abridged from the story 'Count Alaric's Lady',
in *Selected Fairy Tales* by Barbara Leonie Picard, published by
Oxford University Press, 1994.

Oxford University Press, Great Clarendon Street, Oxford OX2 6DP

Oxford New York
Athens Auckland Bangkok Bogota Buenos Aires Calcutta
Cape Town Chennai Dar es Salaam Delhi Florence Hong Kong Istanbul
Karachi Kuala Lumpur Madrid Melbourne Mexico City Mumbai
Nairobi Paris Sao Paulo Singapore Taipei Tokyo Toronto Warsaw

and associated companies in
Berlin Ibadan

Oxford is a trade mark of Oxford University Press

British Library Cataloguing in Publication Data
Data available

ISBN 0 19 279879 0 (hardback)
ISBN 0 19 272354 5 (paperback)

Typeset in Palatino
by Mary Tudge (Typesetting Services)

Printed and bound in Portugal by Edições ASA

THE
MIDSUMMER
BRIDE

Barbara Leonie Picard
Illustrated by Alan Marks

Oxford University Press

EARLY ONE MIDSUMMER'S DAY, Count Alaric rode
from his castle. In a meadow he saw a maiden, barefoot,
wearing a green gown. Her hair was flaxen and her eyes were
golden-green.

When Alaric asked her, 'What is your name?', she replied,
'I do not know.'

'Where are you from?'

'I do not know,' she said again.

'Where are you going to?' Alaric asked.

'I do not know,' she answered. Yet she did not seem
distressed, and she smiled, but as though she smiled at
something half-remembered, rather than at him.

Alaric took her to his castle and called her Catherine, and because he loved her and she was willing, he married her. But whenever he looked into her eyes, she seemed to be thinking of something far away.

When there were festivities and dancing, Catherine never took part. And though he longed to dance with her, Alaric respected her wish.

One day he found her alone, dancing. 'You dance so gracefully,' he said. 'Why will you never dance with me?'

'I never want to dance,' she replied.

'But you were dancing a moment ago.'

'I heard the music. I had to dance.'

'There was no music,' Alaric said.

'There was,' she insisted.

'Can you still hear it?'

She listened before shaking her head. 'No, it is silent now.'

'Tell me, Catherine, are you happy with me?'

'Of course I am happy,' she answered.

But still Alaric saw that strange look in her eyes.

A year passed, all but a day, since he had found her, and the day before midsummer's eve, Alaric had to go on a journey.

The next evening, Alaric rode home. He rode all night because he wished to be with Catherine at that very hour they had met, twelve months before. Towards dawn, as he passed the meadow where he had first seen her, he heard music and saw figures dancing in the moonlight: pale faces with flying hair, garments of green, and bare white feet.

'It is the fairy people dancing on midsummer's eve,' thought Alaric, riding closer. Then he saw that one among them wore crimson. 'It is my Catherine! I have often seen her wearing that gown. The fairy people have lured her from the castle. I must save her.' He urged his horse forward, but when it came nearer the fairy people, it took fright and bolted. Three miles away he calmed it and turned for home, yet before he reached the place where the dancers had been, a cock crew. The meadow was deserted.

Back at the castle Alaric ran to Catherine's room. She was in bed, asleep. She awoke and smiled.

'Is all well with you?' he asked.

'Of course all is well,' she said.

'What did you do last night?' Alaric asked.

'I slept. What else should I have done?' She smiled again. 'I am tired. Wake me when the sun is high.'

'I was mistaken,' thought Alaric. 'She was not there.' But then he noticed her crimson gown. Its hem was wet, as though dragged through dew. Alaric said no more of the matter, yet every time he looked into Catherine's eyes, he was sad.

Then Alaric remembered Magda, the wise woman who lived on the heath, and thought that she might help him. He went to her with his trouble. 'Tell me what ails my Catherine, good Magda, for I love her dearly.'

With pity, Magda answered, 'Count Alaric, your wife is of the fairy people. Away from them she forgets most of her old life. That is why she can tell you nothing about herself. So long as she has the least memory of her past, she will never be wholly yours. On midsummer's eve she will always have to dance with her people, and one day she may not return.'

'Is there no way I can make her wholly mine? No way I can make her forget her people?' Alaric asked.

Magda said, 'Offer her a love so perfect that it leaves no room in her mind for any other memories. Then you will be able to look into her eyes and see that she is thinking only of you and of herself and of your life together.'

'My love for her is perfect. I love her with all my heart. I would die for her!' Alaric exclaimed.

'There must be something lacking,' said Magda. 'If your love for her were perfect, she would be wholly yours.'

From that day Alaric was even kinder to Catherine than before—if that were possible. Yet whenever he looked into her eyes, he saw that he had failed.

Next midsummer's eve, at dusk, Catherine slipped from the castle in a gown of blue velvet. The further she went, the louder grew the fairy music in her ears. Alaric, watching secretly, buckled on his sword and rode after her.

In the meadow he heard the music and saw the fairy people. Catherine was among them, her feet bare and her flaxen hair hanging about her shoulders.

Alaric dismounted and came nearer. As he watched her
dancing gaily, he felt his heart would break. 'She must be
mine,' he thought. 'I will take her from them, no matter how.'
He drew his sword, stepped in among the dancers, and seized
her arm.

The fairy people scattered into a group a short way off.
She would have gone with them, but he held her fast.
'Catherine,' he said, 'I have come to fetch you home.'

She struggled, while the fairy people stretched out their
arms like white moonbeams, calling, 'Come back to us,
our sister.'

Finding she could not break free, she became cunning.
She smiled. 'My people wait for me. Dear husband, let me join
the dancing. When it is over, I shall return.'

'No. If I let you go, you may never return.'

The fairy people fluttered their arms and garments of
green. 'Our sister, come back to us.'

She knelt and lifted her face to his. Her eyes were wet. 'The fairy people have no tears, but you have taught me how to weep.'

Then, when she knew her pleading could not move him, she leapt to her feet and cried, 'Give me your strength, my people!'

They broke from their group and encircled her and Alaric.
'Be strong, our sister. Be strong and come back to us.'

She became a tree with the wind in its branches, Alaric's
hand clasping its trunk. The wind blew to tear it from him.
But he flung aside his sword and clung to the tree, and at last
the wind died down.

The ring of fairy people swayed nearer. 'Be fierce, our sister. Be fierce and come back to us.'

She became a vixen which writhed in his arms and bit to the bone. But he held it until it was quiet.

The fairy circle drew closer. 'Be wild, our sister. Be wild and come back to us.'

She became a salmon, twisting to slip from his grasp. But he gripped it firmly until it gasped.

The fairy feet stepped nearer. 'Be formless, our sister. Be formless and come back to us.'

She became water to trickle through his fingers. But he cupped it in his hands.

The fairy voices were closer. 'Be swift, our sister. Be swift and come back to us.'

She became a breath of wind, to fly away for ever. But he clasped it to his heart.

The fairy people pressed nearer. 'Be burning, our sister. Be burning and come back to us.'

She became a tongue of flame that scorched him.

He thought, 'If I can hold her until dawn, she will be partly mine for another year.'

Then she took once again her own shape and sank down at his feet. 'You are too strong for me. I cannot escape,' she said.

A wail rose from the fairy people and their circle scattered. Their garments merged with the grass. Their hair was like a mist to hide them and their voices grew dim.

Alaric saw a streak of yellow in the east. 'It is almost dawn,' he thought. 'She will be with me for another year.' Then he looked where she crouched. 'Catherine, if you stay with me, will you remember your people and be sad?'

'I shall only partly remember,' she replied. 'I shall regret them faintly, and always know that there is something I have lost, but not what it is.'

'If you returned to your people, would you remember our life together and regret that it was past?' Alaric asked.

'I would remember nothing of our life together. I would forget you utterly.'

For a while Alaric stood in silence, then he sighed and said, 'I do not wish you to have even a moment's sorrow. Return to your people and be happy.' He freed her wrist and she went towards the fairy people who held out their hands to her.

In the distance the first cock crew. 'It is dawn,' thought Alaric. 'They will take her away and I shall never see her again.' He ran to his horse and did not look back, for he could not bear to see the meadow empty where his Catherine had been.

Alaric galloped blindly by fields and woods, not caring where his horse carried him, for he was thinking, 'I have lost her. I can never be happy again in all my life.'

An hour later, he found himself on the road to his castle. Along the track trudged a figure in a blue velvet gown. 'Catherine!' he called.

Joyfully she turned. 'Oh, Alaric, I cannot walk another step, I am so weary. And, see, I have lost my shoes. I awoke in a meadow, all alone. I was so afraid. Did you ride out to find me? And were you afraid too?'

'I rode out to find you. And I was afraid.'

He lifted her on to his horse, and when he looked into her eyes, he saw that she was thinking only of him and of herself and of their life together.

And in that moment Count Alaric knew that love is perfect only when it will give up even the thing which it loves, for that thing's sake.